Pompom

by

Michaela Morgan

Illustrated by Dee Shulman

You do not need to read this page – just get on with the book!

First published in 2000 in Great Britain by
Barrington Stoke Ltd
www.barringtonstoke.co.uk

This edition published 2006

ISBN-10: 1-84299-444-1
ISBN-13: 978-1-84299-444-3

Printed in Great Britain by Bell and Bain Ltd

MEET THE AUTHOR - MICHAELA MORGAN

What is your favourite animal?
Dogs, cats, elephants, penguins and hamsters
What is your favourite boy's name?
David
What is your favourite girl's name?
Mel
What is your favourite food?
Chips and chocolate (not together!)
What is your favourite music?
Pop music
What is your favourite hobby?
Daydreaming

MEET THE ILLUSTRATOR - DEE SHULMAN

What is your favourite animal?
Stick insects
What is your favourite boy's name?
Charlie Bucket
What is your favourite girl's name?
Cruella de Vil
What is your favourite food?
Banana custard
What is your favourite music?
My son on the violin and
my daughter on guitar
What is your favourite hobby?
Stopping our kitten climbing
up the curtains

Contents

Chapter 1
Nothing Special

Everyone wants to be something special. Some kids want to be a pop singer or a footballer or an astronaut.

What I wanted was for all the other kids to like me, Paul Bridges. Don't get me wrong. They don't hate me or anything like that. They just never notice me. I'm not all that popular or unpopular. That's the trouble.

I'm not all that anything. I'm just not all that special.

Sometimes I wonder what it would be like to be like Dean. Dean always has a crowd round him.

He could make them all laugh. He could make a joke. He could play a trick. He could score a goal. He was brilliant at all sports. He was not afraid of anything or anybody.

I was. I was afraid of everything and everybody. I was afraid when Dean and his gang made fun of me. They knew it. That's why they picked on me. No one ever picked on Dean.

Then Mum promised an old friend that I'd look after her dog for a few weeks. When she told me, I was pretty excited. At last here was something interesting, something special that I could talk about – that I could boast about.

"My Mum says it's a special dog ... it's won prizes ... it's a champion," I told my class. "Mrs Norris, the owner, is going to Australia to visit her son and she chose me to look after it because I'm sensible. It's a very valuable dog."

"What sort of a dog is it, Paul?" Miss Taylor asked me.

"Well, I'm not quite sure," I admitted. "I've never seen it – but my Mum says it's a champion. It's won loads of cups."

DOGS

Bloodhound

Can be trained to track and trail.
Good at smelling.

German Shepherd/Alsatian

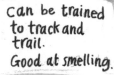

Intelligent dog. Can be trained to help the police.

Labrador

A loyal breed of dog sometimes trained to guide the blind.

Sheepdog

Hard working dogs. Can be trained to round up sheep.

"Maybe you can do your project on dogs," said Miss Taylor. "There are some good books on dogs in the library," she said. "Have a look at them."

So that's what I did. I went to the library.

I spent the rest of the afternoon working on my project and imagining myself with one of these amazing dogs. Some of the other kids took an interest in my dog too.

And when Miss Taylor said we could write a poem or a story quite a few of us wrote about dogs. This was mine.

I want a dog
by Paul Bridges

I want a dog
Any sort of dog
A watchdog
a sheepdog
a guard dog
a gun dog
a work dog
a fun dog
but I want a dog!

I want a dog
Any sort of dog
A tall dog
a small dog
a l o n g dog
a STRONG dog
a dog to race with
a dog to chase with
a fierce and loyal trusty DOG!

Dean wrote one too. He read his out:

I'd have a pit bull terrier
I'd call it **'BLOOD.'**
It would be a fighting dog
YES IT WOULD/
It would bare its teeth
and snarl and growl
stand back and SHAKE
BLOOD is on the prowl!!!

Then Dean growled at me and laughed when I jumped. All his mates laughed too.

****

Everyone wanted to know all about my mystery champion dog.

"Can we come round to your house and see it? Can we walk it with you? Can I help train it?" they all said at once.

I felt great you know – really special.

Chapter 2
Dream Dog

I could hardly wait to get home. I kept imagining myself showing off my new dog.

I'd train it. I'd teach it tricks. I'd race it. I'd teach it to play footy. I'd have it rounding up. I'd have it seeking out, attacking and defending. I'd set it on any bully and save all the little kids (and myself). I'd have it track down my lost swimming kit before I got into trouble about it. I'd teach it to fetch tennis balls, cricket balls, footballs. I would be so good the other kids would probably want me to join the team.

"Oh please ... we need you!" all the little kids would beg.

My dreams filled my head all the way home.

I banged on my front door. I couldn't wait to get home and see my dream dog. Mum opened the door.

I raced in and found ...

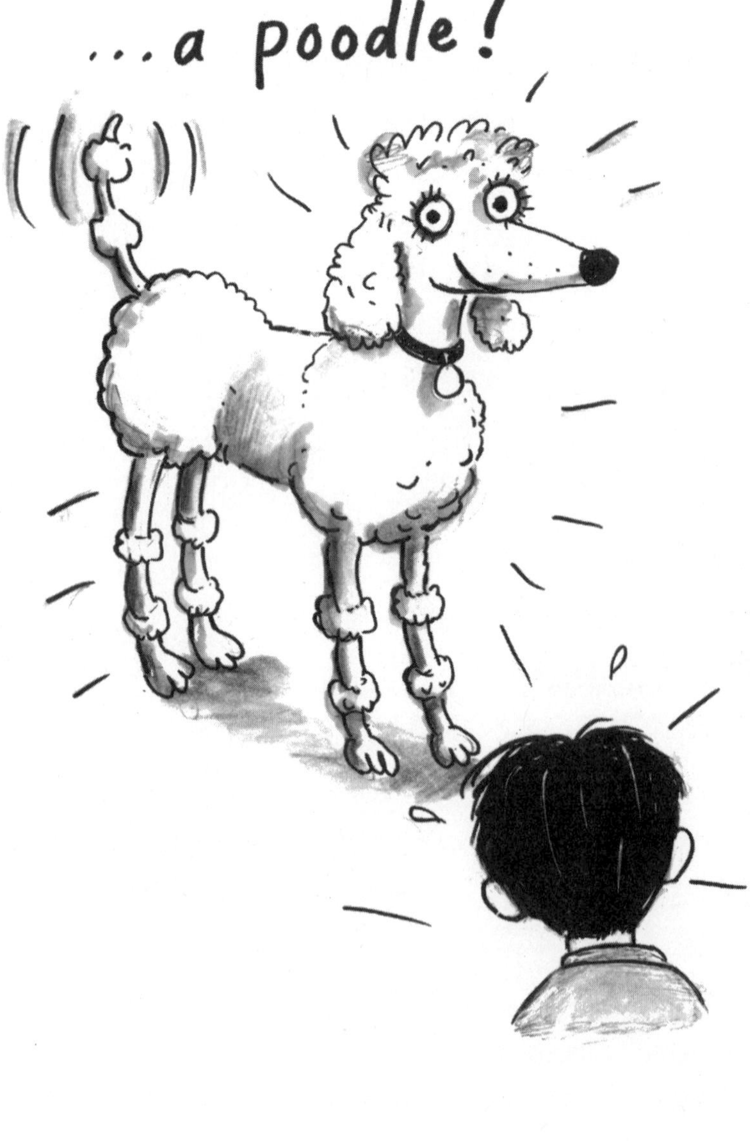
...a poodle!

"She's called Pompom," said Mum, "and she's very quiet – no trouble at all. I promised you'd look after her carefully. Keep her looking nice and don't get her too tired or over-excited. OK?"

It was not OK at all. "It looks silly," I said.

"I've told you before – you should never judge by looks," said Mum. "She's a lovely dog – and I promised you'd look after her. A promise is a promise."

You've never seen a dog as soppy as this one. She (SHE!) was white, bald in places, fluffy in others. She had a stupid sort of pompom of a tail. She was about as fierce as ... a feather. As strong as ... a snowflake. She had all the courage of ... a custard.

"After tea you can take her out," said Mum.

"Er ... not tonight, Mum, I've got to ... do some homework."

"Homework! Well, I've never heard THAT before. You must take her out sometime tonight anyway."

I put it off as long as I could. I was hoping it would get dark but it was still light as day when Mum got tough with me.

What a wally I felt walking down the street with a fluffy poodle. I sneaked down all the back streets and tried to keep out of sight. I kept Pompom on her lead and whenever anyone came near, I quickly ducked into a doorway. She trotted beside me looking up at me, keen to please. I dragged her along so quickly her feet barely touched the ground.

Luck was with me – I made it home without meeting anyone I knew.

Chapter 3
Saturday

The next day was Saturday. I tried to stay in bed as long as I could. I was hoping Mum would get fed up and take the dog out herself. No such luck.

"By the way, Paul," said Mum, "if you have any trouble getting Pompom to come back to you in the park, wave this hanky at her. That's what Mrs Norris, her owner, did and it worked every time," and with that Mum handed me a little, white lace hanky.

"Thanks, Mum," I groaned.

Saturday morning in the park! I was bound to meet some kids I knew there. Dean was always there with his footy crowd on Saturdays. I could just imagine what he'd say if he saw me with a fluffy poodle and a little lace hanky. I would never live it down.

I tried every excuse to get out of it. "I've got a pain in my stomach ... I'm too tired ... I've lost my shoes ... got to tidy my room ..."

But Mum was having none of it.

TAKE THAT DOG OUT NOW!!!

I thought of making a disguise for Pompom somehow. But how? I thought of dyeing her white fur black or grey or brown with shoe polish. Maybe if she was a bit darker she'd look more like a real dog.

But the only colour polish in our house was blue and I thought that might make her stand out even more. Maybe I could rub her with mud? But nothing could hide her ridiculous shape.

In the end, I hid at the bottom of the garden while I zipped my coat round her. I'd read somewhere that some dogs do wear winter coats. But perhaps an anorak wasn't quite right. She looked very odd. Still, it was the best I could think of.

Pompom was puzzled. She looked up at me as if to tell me that she didn't think this was a very good idea.

She couldn't understand that I'd decided to tell everyone that she was a rare rainforest dog who couldn't stand cold temperatures. She could hardly ever come out of doors and when she did, she had to wear a coat.

So this is what I told everyone.

Chapter 4
The Rare Rainforest Dog

The other kids looked a bit suspicious when I told them. "It's a rare rainforest dog."

Still, I might have got away with it if Pompom hadn't spotted another dog ... and raced after it.

Off flew the anorak. Pompom could be seen for what she really was. A great big, silly, soppy, fluffy, female poodle.

"Some fighting dog!" sneered Dean. "Did you hear that bark! Or was it a squeak?"

"She could probably run better if she didn't have a leg stuck in my anorak," I tried to stick up for her.

I shouldn't have bothered. It made it worse.

"SHE!! Oh, my. It's a little girlie dog. A curly, girlie dog."

This had really made Dean's day. He liked nothing better than to find someone to tease. I tried my best to look as if I didn't care. "I must not blush!" I told myself.

But I could feel my ears growing from pinky warm ... to red hot ... to boiling scarlet.

Quite a crowd had gathered by now. I suddenly began to understand what it meant when people said they wished the ground would open up and swallow them.

As this wasn't likely to happen, I thought I'd just better get away as quickly as possible. "Pompom," I called.

Mistake.

That gave them something else to laugh at.

"Pompom! Pompom!" Dean started to mince around and mimic me.

The others started to chant along with him. "Pompom! Pompom!" in mimsy little voices. "Come on little Pompom! Come to Daddykins!"

I called to Pompom again. Of course the stupid dog ignored me and I had to get the little lace hanky out and wave it.

Do I have to describe the jeering, the mocking, the nudging, the sniggering and giggling? Why don't you just imagine it?

I've got enough to do catching this dog and dragging it out of the park. *And* putting up with all the other kids laughing and pointing at me.

I've enough to do trying to stop my legs trembling and my face and ears burning.

I've enough to do making sure that that awful pricking feeling in my eyes doesn't turn into tears.

Chapter 5
Roderick

Outside the park I wandered round a bit, carefully avoiding any streets where I might be recognised. I couldn't face going home yet. They'd be bound to notice I'd been crying – well nearly crying I mean.

I was sitting on a low wall outside some shops when ...

"What a DARLING poodle!" said a voice from behind me.

I looked around. I was expecting it to be one of my so-called friends sending me up. But it was that posh Mrs Rawley taking an enormous basket of flowers to her equally enormous car.

"You simply MUST show her in our dog show. I'll ask Roderick to bring you an entry form. You are one of Roderick's little friends, aren't you?"

There are many things people could say I was – cowardly, stupid, even boring – but no way was I 'one of Roderick's little friends'.

Whenever I was having a really bad day – like today for example – I could always make myself feel better by saying to myself, 'Things could be worse – you could be Roderick.'

To be Roderick Rawley (yes, really – you try saying it fast) was worse than being a wally, worse than being a twerp, a jerk, a nerd or a twit. If anyone at our school really wanted to insult you they'd say, 'He's turning into a right little Roderick, isn't he?'

Roderick was the new boy at our school. His Mum was always hanging around him telling him to be careful. She said he was 'delicate'.

We said he was a wimp. It adds up to the same thing. He didn't know how to play football. He said he got tired if he ran.

In swimming lessons he shivered on the steps in the shallow end. His teeth chattered and his skin went all blue and goosepimply. His Mum sent him in with armbands and made him wear them years after we'd all stopped wearing them. He didn't half look soft.

He had arrived one day, not like all the other kids, but driven to the door in his family's big car. His Dad and Mum even came into the classroom with him and shook Miss Taylor's hand.

We'd all been at our school since we were four or five. We had our friends, our groups, our gangs all sorted out.

shirt
and
tie

blazer

SHORTS!!!!

long
grey socks

briefcase

shiny black
lace-up
shoes

He didn't fit in at all. He talked posh. He looked pale. He couldn't fight for toffee. And he wore weird, weird clothes – shiny, black lace-up shoes, long, grey socks, shorts, a shirt and tie, a blazer – not the sort of things we wear!

"Sit down," Miss Taylor had said, "and let's add you to the register. Now your full name is ... ?"

"Wodewick Wawey," he said.

Oh no, it was too much! A name like that and he couldn't say the letter 'R'.

And later we found that he wasn't too good at 'L' or 'W' either.

"I beg your pardon," said Miss Taylor. She hadn't been able to hear over all the giggling.

"Lodelick Lawley" he said. And each time he tried to get his name right, it got worse and worse and we found it funnier and funnier – until he blushed and started to stammer.

"Crybaby Bawley," hissed Dean and that was it.

From that day on it was Roderick's fate to be laughed at, whatever he said or did. He was always the one who was left out of everything. He was the one you were always glad not to be.

So you see, even though I was stuck with a poodle, things could have been worse.

Chapter 6
Worse and Worse

So things could have been worse. But not much worse.

Here I am huddled in the doorway of a flower shop. Stuck between a basket of flowers, a poodle and Mrs Rawley.

I am trying to be invisible while Mrs Rawley rummages around in her handbag muttering, "I'm sure I've got one of the forms in here ... really the sooner you fill one in the better ... now where can it be ..." she prattled and patted Pompom.

Pompom beamed up at her.

They really had taken to each other.

I was frantic. I was trying to think of an excuse so I could get away. But just when you think life is really terrible, do you know what happens? It gets worse.

What could be worse you ask? Well, look down the street. What do you see? Yep. Dean and his footy crowd coming round the corner.

"Can't seem to find the thing anywhere ..." said Mrs Rawley, still rummaging through her many-pocketed handbag. "I'll have to get one from home."

She opened the back door of the car and put the flowers inside. As she did that, Dean came round the corner. He had his hands in his pockets and his head down, he hadn't seen me ... yet.

I took action. I jumped into the car, dragging a startled Pompom behind me.

"OK," I said. "Let's go!" I slammed the door and crouched down behind the flowers. To be seen with a basket of flowers, a poodle and posh Mrs Rawley was more than my street cred could stand.

"Oh well ... yes ... of course ... I suppose so ..." Mrs Rawley was puzzled. She blinked vaguely and got into the car.

Pompom sat up smartly and wagged her pompom tail. I slid down behind the flowers.

"Good morning, boys," trilled Mrs Rawley. She waved at Dean and his mob.

Oh no! She was attracting attention to us. But it turned out to be the right thing to do. Faced with the possibility of a chat with Mrs Rawley, Dean and his gang scuttled off into a sweet shop.

Mrs Rawley started the car and we were off.

Chapter 7
At Home with Roderick

"You really shouldn't just jump into cars like that," said Mrs Rawley. "I know I'm not exactly a stranger but still ..."

She handed me a mobile phone. "Phone home and ask if you can come over to my house. You can collect the form and have tea with Roderick. You can play all day if Mummy agrees."

I dialled home. 'Mummy' agreed. So I had a day with a poodle, Mrs Rawley and Roderick to look forward to.

"Just make yourself at home," said Mrs Rawley.

Anywhere less like my home would be hard to imagine. My home would probably fit into two of their downstairs rooms. Their garden was like a park.

Roderick was out there sitting on a bench and half-heartedly balancing a football on his foot. He looked up as I walked towards him.

"One of your friends has come over to play!" said Mrs Rawley.

Isn't that nice?

Roderick and I eyed each other uneasily.

I'd never really had much to do with him at school. He stayed pretty quiet in the background. I went along with the others when they laughed at him. The silence stretched between us. Something had to give. It was me.

"I'm picking up a form for some dog show from your Mum. She says I should enter this dog." I pointed to Pompom and waited for Roderick to snigger just like all the others who had seen her.

But Roderick just glanced at Pompom then tickled her ears. "Nice dog," he said. "You should stand a good chance of winning a prize with her. First prize is £50 you know."

£50! Wow! Maybe Pompom wasn't altogether bad news!

"Course it's not just the looks that count," said Roderick. "There's a whole lot of other tests too. Is it trained?"

"Don't know. It's not really my dog. I'm just looking after the soppy thing."

Roderick patted Pompom. She snuggled against him gratefully. "It's a good dog," he said. "Pity they clip them like that. It makes them look a bit soppy – underneath it they're really good dogs. They're brave hunters. Intelligent too. And good-natured and loyal."

Pompom leant against Roderick, gazing at him with adoring eyes. She licked his hand as if to show her intelligence, good nature and loyalty. She gave a little yip as if to say 'see it's all true!'. She waved her pompom tail from side to side and skipped around him on her little pompom feet. She certainly didn't look like a brave hunter!

Roderick threw a stick for her. Like a shot, Pompom was after it. Seconds later she was back. She dropped the stick at our feet and looked pleased with herself.

"She'd be a good dog to train," said Roderick.

I took the stick and threw it. I threw much further than Roderick and couldn't resist giving him a look to make sure he'd noticed. He had. The stick went off into the trees, out of sight.

Pompom raced after it. I sprinted as fast as I could after her but I couldn't keep up. I got to the trees in time to see her leaping over a tree stump. Then shaking herself and panting happily, she dropped the stick at my feet.

"Not bad!" I said turning to Roderick.

But I'd forgotten what a pathetic runner he was. He was still metres away. Finally he arrived, breathless and a little blue.

"Pompom's really fast," I boasted, "not like you!" I couldn't resist having a bit of a go at him. "You don't half take your time," I added.

Roderick had flopped on the floor by now. He lay like a fish gasping for breath.

"Oh, don't be such a wimp ..." I started to say but I didn't finish.

A girl was running towards us. She pushed me to one side and leant over Roderick.

"I'm OK," he panted. "Don't fuss," and he struggled to sit up.

"We'll go back to the house," said the girl. "Take your time."

What was going on?

Chapter 8
The Scrapbook

Back at the house Roderick was whisked away by Mrs Rawley and I was left with the girl.

"I'm Rachel," she said. "Rick's – Roderick's – sister. You must be one of his friends from his new school."

"Paul," I muttered my name. I didn't add that I wasn't one of Roderick's friends. That he had no friends at our school. I didn't have the chance to add anything. Rachel was what my Mum would call a chatterbox.

On and on she chattered with hardly a pause for breath. "Mum and Dad were really pleased when Rick told them how well he was doing at his new school and how friendly you all were. He'd had such an awful time at his last place. Everyone there was sports mad and of course with his dodgy heart he couldn't join in. And he'd missed so much school with all the time he's spent in hospital so he could never catch up or fit in ..."

On and on she went and bit by bit I made sense of it. It all became completely clear when I saw the scrapbook.

BROUGHTON HIGH SCHOOL
CARRINGTON ROAD
EDINBURGH
EH4 1EG

So this was the Roderick that Dean had made fun of.

And I was as bad as Dean – maybe even worse. I knew what it felt like to be picked on but I'd joined in. I felt ashamed.

Chapter 9
Making Friends

Roderick came back to us after a while, he looked much better now.

"Rick would like you not to say anything about this at school," Rachel had whispered to me. "He doesn't like being picked out for special treatment."

We all made a start on training Pompom. Roderick knew exactly what to do and me and

Rachel did all the running around and lifting and stuff. Pompom was really quick to learn.

"She's used to being in shows," said Roderick. "Look how well she walks to heel. But she doesn't seem to have done any of the intelligence training."

He explained the tricks that she would need to do and showed me some pictures. Rachel and I set out seesaws of wood and barrels and little jumps and we made a tunnel out of an old tent. We spent the whole afternoon training Pompom. To tell the truth I enjoyed it.

I was running alongside Pompom watching her leap and twirl in the air. Roderick was sitting on the ground. I looked towards him to see if he'd noticed how high she was jumping. He had. And there was something in his eyes. A sort of wishing. I could tell he was wishing he could run and jump too.

I suddenly realised that there was more than one way of being brave.

I went back a couple of evenings that week – well, every evening that week and the next week ... and the next.

We taught Pompom all the tricks. We even taught her how to stand and guard. She would stand exactly where we told her and she'd bare her teeth and growl like a real guard dog.

I told myself I only went there because it was a safe place to exercise Pompom without meeting Dean and his lot, but I was also finding out that the more I got to know Roderick, the more I got to like him.

The thing was, we were friends after school and behind his garden walls, but back in school I didn't have the nerve to admit it.

When everyone was teasing him, I didn't actually join in now. But I didn't stick up for him either. Which is why I felt so bad that Friday afternoon.

Chapter 10
Showdown

For some reason, Mum had decided to meet me from school. For some reason, she'd decided to bring Pompom with her. Then she'd decided to pop into the supermarket – which left me standing outside with the poodle.

Me – standing with a poodle in the middle of the High Street, just along from my school. I expect you can guess what happened next.

Along came Dean and his gang.

"Waiting for Mummy are we? Got our little doggy to look after?" he mocked. "Got our little lace hanky have we, in case of emergency?"

"Don't need it now," I muttered, "I've trained her."

I just stared at my feet. Better not to get involved, I thought. Try not to blush. Look cool, I thought.

But there was no stopping Dean once he'd started.

He grabbed hold of Pompom's tail and started to flick at the pompom on the end of it and fall about laughing. He perched his empty crisp packet on her tail. He roared with laughter as Pompom wagged it madly trying to get the crisp packet off.

Then he caught hold of Pompom's lead. Pompom looked alarmed and yipped. "We'll soon teach her who's boss, won't we gang?"

The rest of his group bleated in agreement.

Pompom looked at me, but what could I do against all of them? It would be madness to take Dean and all his gang on. I didn't know what to do.

Then out of the supermarket came Roderick and his sister. They glanced at us, saw Pompom struggling to get away from Dean. Saw me standing there red-faced and shaking.

Roderick didn't hesitate. He faced Dean and shouted, "Hey you!"

Several shoppers looked to see what was going on.

Dean and his gang turned on Roderick. Dean flicked Roderick's hair. "Ooh, ooh, look it's little Roderick!"

The gang's attention was on Roderick now. They forgot about Pompom. I waited for my chance to grab her lead back.

Rachel was looking puzzled. Were these her brother's friends?

"Ooh, got our girlfriend with us have we?" Now they just turned on Rachel and waited for her to blush.

But she snorted and turned to her brother. "Who are these *little* boys?" she said.

Dean looked stunned. He looked even more stunned when Roderick said quite calmly, "Oh, they're no one to worry about." Then quite calmly, quite deliberately, he took Pompom's lead from them.

"Guard! Pompom!" he said.

Pompom obediently bared her teeth and growled. Dean took a step back.

"That's showing him," said an old lady passing by. "Should be ashamed of himself," she added.

Several other shoppers tut-tutted their agreement. Dean was going pink.

"Frightened by a poodle, Dean?" Roderick enquired calmly.

"Course not!" stammered Dean.

No one believed him. Behind him one of his own gang sniggered. Dean stuffed his hands in his pockets and turned away. "Got no time to waste with you," he shouted as he moved off. "Got better things to do." He broke into a run. His gang scattered after him.

Rachel laughed – a loud, clear, ringing laugh, like music.

****

All the rest of that term we worked with Pompom. She didn't win the competition – but she did come third and Rick says that's excellent for a first try.

"She'll do even better next year," he said.

We've planned it all out. Mrs Norris, Pompom's real owner, says I can take Pompom out any time I want. She was really pleased with the way I'd looked after her dog.

I became best mates with Pompom – and with Rick and Rachel. We've made a great training course for Pompom in their garden.

Some of the other kids have started coming to watch. One of Dean's gang even brings his dog to join in.

Dean came along once too. He just watched and cracked the odd joke but we didn't mind. He's not all that bad when you get to know him. My Mum says you should never judge by looks.

"The strongest people are frightened inside," she says, "and those who seem to be weak may be really strong."

I never used to understand what she was talking about – but now I think I'm beginning to.

Barrington Stoke would like to thank all its readers for commenting on the manuscript before publication and in particular:

Rosemary Anderson
Alice Baker
Nigel Brown
Lindsay Fraser
Zara Frost
Gerogina Jansz
David Jones
Mrs C Loven
Natasha Marshall
Caroline Morris
Christine Ostler
Lizzie Pace
Emma Standley
Kirstie Wilson

Become a Consultant!

Would you like to give us feedback on our titles before they are published? Contact us at the email address below – we'd love to hear from you!

info@barringtonstoke.co.uk
www.barringtonstoke.co.uk

Also by the same author ...

Letter from America

Tommo's fed up. His teacher has had another of her ideas. She wants everyone in the class to have a penpal. Tommo knows it's going to be boring, boring, BORING. But he's in for a big surprise! Share Tommo's sad times and his happy times – and meets Shelley who raps, rhymes and jokes in her letters from America.

You can order *Letter from America* directly from our website at www.barringtonstoke.co.uk

Also by the same author ...

Buddies

Friends to the end?

Tommo's mum has walked out. He's in so much trouble at school that he's stopped going at all. The only thing he looks forward to is Shelley's crazy letters from America. But can Shelley really help Tommo – and can the penpals stay best buddies?

More exciting titles!

Lift Off
by Hazel Townson

Ronnie hates sports! So he knows the right place to be for Sports Day – at home, watching telly.

But there's a man he doesn't know in his house and he's taking the telly away. Ronnie's got to start running now – for his life!

You can order _Lift Off_ directly from our website at www.barringtonstoke.co.uk

More exciting titles!

Life Line
by Rosie Rushton

Skid doesn't want to tell people what his home is really like. It's a lot better to make stuff up – until he gets found out! Now Skid's in big trouble – can his new friend Cassie help him get away with it?

You can order *Life Line* directly from our website at www.barringtonstoke.co.uk